Elective Affinities

David Adjmi

SAMUELFRENCH.COM
SAMUELFRENCH-LONDON.CO.UK

ELECTIVE AFFINITES was commissioned by the Royal Court Theatre. premiered at the Royal Shakespeare Company, Stratford on Avon, in October 2005. The performance was directed by Dominic Cooke.

ALICE HAUPTMANN . . . . Suzanne Burden

The production transferred to the Soho Theatre, London in April 2006 with the same cast and creative team.

ELECTIVE AFFINITES received its New York premiere at Soho Repertory Theatre in a co-production with Piece by Piece Productions and Rising Phoenix Repertory. The opening night was December 2, 2011. The performance was directed by Dominic Cooke, with sets by Louisa Thompson, costumes by Susan Hilferty, lights by Mark Barton, and sound by Matt Tierney. The Production Stage Manager was Tom Taylor.

ALICE HAUPTMANN . . . . Zoe Caldwell

CHARACTERS

ALICE HAUPTMANN – a witty, civilized, and highly sophisticated octogenarian

SETTING

The apartment of Alice Hauptmann. *ELECTIVE AFFINITES* can be performed in site specific locations.

TIME

Present day

*(**ALICE** stands alone, addressing the audience. A chair, a tea service, a plate of expensive chocolates. She's very wealthy, dressed opulently – she's of the Brooke Astor, Gloria Vanderbilt ilk – almost of another era. She's very charming.)*

ALICE. *(chatty, very conversational)*

And so he asked us "Are you going with something big or something small?" And John said well maybe small is best, because then it won't take up much space. And I said, no - *no*, it's got to be *big*, because the *world* is big, and I want to see that bigness in the confines of this *one* room in this *one* house; I want it confined to *one room* the vastness of all the world, every latitude and longitude imaginable, I want it squeezed into *one* shape, and I want to look at it whenever I *want*.

And John was just *galled* – and he stormed out of the room with his briefcase. And the artist, he sort of gulped, he was a little daunted I could tell, but I think it turned out alright. I mean, we're pleased with it. I mean, it's this very big, black, hulking…*mass*. It's a little terrifying. We're sort of…afraid. Of it. And John is very cross with me.

(She regards the sculpture.)

It seems sort of African to me. Or *Iberian*, maybe. I've never actually been to Africa. Or Iberia for that matter.

(beat)

To tell you the truth, I've never been anywhere, not outside my own country. But I've been to *museums*, I've been to *lots* of museums. I like museums better than I like art! I think they're very civilized. I've never been to Africa, but I've been to the Guggenheim. People say to me but you seem well traveled and I say, I *seem* it, but I'm *not*. I read books and I watch movies. But I don't like airplanes. I prefer to stay where I am and have the world come to me. It's very arrogant I know; I'm *terrible*.

(beat; then excitedly:)

Oh, and I watch the *Nature* Channel – have you ever watched that? You can see animals eat each other *alive!* *(She laughs maniacally.)* Can you *believe* it, they actually show this – I mean, it's almost *pornographic!* And, it's not just insects or grasshoppers, but big bloody animals, with tendons coming apart, and blood and gore, my *god.*

(pours tea into a cup)

My husband, John, he travels a lot. He's in Japan right now doing business. He's very cross with me, as I said – he doesn't like that thing – that's what he calls it "that thing." Or sometimes "das ding" – he's German so sometimes he says it in German – and that's how it is in German, "Das ding."

He's afraid of it, John is. A few nights ago he said to me "Alice, it's growing, I think it's growing." I told him he was being silly. He said "Either *it's* growing, or I'm *shrinking*". You know, Germans are such fraidy cats, they really are. The Germans themselves have a word for this…

(beat)

I don't know what it *is*, but I'm sure there is one.

(adds sugar and milk to tea)

Maybe they don't have a word for it – I don't know anything anymore. So John is cross with me, everyone is so cross around me, but people are just peevish these days. I mean, don't you find that? That people are so peevish? For example my girlfriend Deirdre – I mean I love her and we've known each other for ages – but she just got *very* recriminatory with me at a dinner party. She said – and she tends to get very annoying when she drinks, I mean she can really get on your nerves – she said "but Alice: how can you justify what you said last week at the benefit about the *tor*turing of political *pris*oners. I mean can you really justify the use of *torture* on political *prisoners?*" And I said "I *wasn't* justifying it." And she said "Well, *Alice* I'm not sure I understood your position. I mean, maybe I misunderstood your position, but from what I gathered you seemed to be really excited about the torturing of political prisoners, and what's *that* about?"

I said to her "Look Deirdre: who wants to use torture? *No one*, that's who. *Nobody* does, it's *unpleasant.* I was merely stating *fact.* I was merely stating that torture *would* be used. That the FBI could, should and *would* use it and that they *will* use *torture.* That's just how it is. And that *any* democracy in a ticking bomb situation would do that, that's just how it is."

She said, "A ticking bomb situation – what's *that?*" I said "You know, like in those films, those horrible action films, when someone plants a bomb on a bus and you have a limited amount of time to defuse the thing but don't know where it is, and you've captured the bomber, and he won't tell you. What are you going to do then?

I'll tell you what you're going to do: you're going to *torture* that man! *Anyone* would – to find out how to *defuse* it? *Anyone* would do that."

"But I could *never* torture *anybody*"

"Not even if your husband's *life* was at stake?"

"No"

"Or your daughter or your grandchild, not even then?"

No, said Deirdre.

I could never. Torture. *Anyone.*

(She takes a short pause, then rolls her eyes. Takes a sip of tea.)

Ezra Pound, you know, that *poet?* He called the space between the two wars

" a parenthesis of peace" Isn't that quaint sounding, "a *parenthesis* of *peace.*" I love that.

Where are we now, do you think? Mid sentence? – or no, mid paragraph, mid *volume?*

I don't know where we are.

My mother used to read his cantos to me before bed. You know, those *cantos?* I didn't know what anything meant, but I *loved* it. My mother was a very great woman. I know everyone says that about their mothers, but in her case it was true. I had a very happy childhood. I remember during world war two I asked my mother "Why are we at war?" She said it was simply because men liked war, that they liked it better than any other subject - they liked wars, violence and sports.

I don't have any children myself… I wanted to – and we tried for a while – we did *try.* And then after a while we stopped trying – or *I* stopped trying. John kept trying, he was testing his, oh, mascu*lin*ity or something.

But I surrendered. I accepted my fate. You know, like one of those gazelles, in the jungle, or the woods, or wherever the hell gazelles live. But it's incredible really, when they're captured by some predator…they just sort of tilt their heads back like this:

(She tilts her head back and a little to the side.)

And this look of peace comes over them, in their eyes, this very…peaceful look… they're saying "*yes,* I accept my fate – *yes,* I'm resigned to the fact that I'm going to die… and I accept that.

(She's gotten a bit dreamy and faraway, maybe even a bit sad, but snaps out of it.)

That was me! I was like one of those gazelles. I accepted my fate and – well that's a very dramatic analogy – I actually have a very nice life. I mean, *I* think it's a nice life.

(Beat; she pops a chocolate in her mouth.)

Or maybe it's horrible. Maybe it's a *horrible* life and I just don't see how horrible it is. But – I mean I *feel* happy. I've always considered myself a happy person. I've always *been* happy, I've always loved life. People say to me "but you're so rich, you must be spiritually empty." And I said, "But I've managed to find spiritual fulfillment in material *things*." For example this tea – now I know this is going to sound dumb, but I just love tea, I love *this* tea – and when I drink it, I feel edified *spiritually*. I really do.

(takes another sip)

It's from Japan, this brand of tea. John brought it home for me — and it's just unbelievably good; and the flavours, they have names like "Good Times" and "Swing Time" and – ha ha – "Time of Your Life" or, or "Happy *Ride*" – something like that I don't know… They don't correspond to any flavors in life, like peach or lemon. It's called "tonal systems." Isn't that a funny name?

(takes another sip)

OH – do you know that *ride*, that *teacup* ride? In *Disneyworld?* Have you ever been there? We went last year, and – say what you will about Disney, and Lion King – "hakuna makata" and all that but – really it was so much *fun*. We just *loved* it, una*bash*edly, we were like two pimply kids. And the teacups are – and I don't know if you've ever seen them – they're just so whimsical. They're *hugely* oversized and you sit inside them and spin around. I love just spinning and spinning. And the children are like little cubes of sugar being stirred around and around…

(beat)

But I'm getting off track now – what was I… oh *yes*, the ticking *bombs* –that's right. Now Deirdre, you must understand, she's a very well meaning person, she's well intentioned, so you can't hate her when she gets really stupid on you. And we're having this incredibly circular argument – "Don't you think it's sort of *bad* to torture people?" "But Deirdre Darling I'm not advocating torture." "But Alice Darling it sounds like you are, and we live in a democracy and don't you think we need to protect our democratic *ideals*?" – and as she was saying this they were playing a nocturne of Chopin's, whom I –

(A nocturne plays softly.)

– love to pieces, so I half listened to her and half to the Chopin:

(as Deirdre:)

"And is it really alright to violate certain ideals with the intention of upholding those ideals, I mean do you really think that's *okay*?" And I said, "*Well* Deirdre, if you *want* to live in a civilized society, then I guess it *has* to be okay, doesn't it." And she turned this sort of ugly pink color. And she said "But that's not civilized *behavior*."

(beat)

And I said, "Well, I think *I'm* civilized. I mean I *try* to be nice... and funny, and smart - I mean, I'm a nice person, don't you think so Deirdre? Don't you think *I'm* nice? Don't you like *me*?"

And she sort of tilted her neck back, and she said of *course* she liked me and not to be ridiculous. And I said, "Because *I've* always liked *you*. Because we're *friends*. And you would never torture *me* and I would never torture *you*. Because we're *friends*. And she said, well that's true. And I said "I would never harm you, Deirdre, or anything you loved. Because we're friends and we love each other. And love is preferential. I *prefer* you to other people." I said "I'm with you right now because I'm rejecting billions and *billions* of other people. I'm rejecting them so I can make space for *you*. And our friendship is meaningful precisely because I reject all these other people. You can't love everyone – except in a general way, and love is too important to be generalized."

(Music fades.)

I thought I expostulated quite well.

(beat)

I mean *I* thought so.

(picks up her teacup and sips)

But I mean this whole discourse on human rights – the whole thing is sort of a joke, isn't it? I mean what sort of conversation *is* this? "But we have our *rights!*" As if *all* human beings have some innate value. As if we're these precious jewels, or individualized snowflakes or something idiotic like that.

I mean does anyone actually *believe* this to be true? or do we just *pretend* to believe it? And if we all are pretending to believe it – *why* are we *doing* it? I mean 'I'm a horrible person' yes I *know* that but I'm *sorry*. I mean the gall, to assume that just because we're *human* we have these *rights*. Yes, it's nice to be *nice* to people, yes, absolutely; it's nice to treat people well, I'm not saying people should be mean to other people. But my god, the laziness, to just *assume* we *all* have some innate value… that this is just some *given*.

I mean, look: If someone flies in an airplane – is it their *right* not to crash? Do people ever say "oh, their rights were violated, their *human rights*, because they *crashed*" No, they don't say it because when you're up in the sky – flying around like that – you're defying *nature*.

And nature is very cruel.

Nature confers no *rights*.

(beat)

I mean, the *hubris!*

(Short pause; she crosses her legs – they are nice legs – she may be showing off a bit. Smoothes her stockings.)

I like hosiery a lot. If I had my druthers I'd buy a box of pantyhose every week.

(beat)

I don't really know what druthers are, do you? Anyway, I doubt I have mine.
HA HA HA HA.

(sips tea; then overly casual:)

So!

That's my situation in a nutshell. Deirdre is cross with me, and John is cross with me too. Oh, John is *furious* with me. He thinks I've become "monstrous" – did I mention that? Well he does, that's what he told me. "Alice," he said, "you are becoming a monster. "Oh am I, John, that's so very interesting", I told him, "as if your forefathers weren't gassing Jews by the millions in the death camps."

(She laughs wildly at this. Then a short pause.)

Maybe that was monstrous of me, to say that to him.
It was, wasn't it?

It was very mean.

But maybe that's what you need to be when you're protecting the thing you love. I love my husband, I love my friends. Other people, I'm indifferent to them.

(beat)

Until they harm me. Until they harm someone I love, or threaten to. Then I'm not indifferent. Then you bracket your normal way of living. Then it's war. You can permit horrible things, torture, murder, genocide and that sort of thing.

(beat)

And everyone is so cross with me, but that's what I think. They say "We don't know what to say, we're grief stricken over what's happened, we're stricken with grief, we don't have the language"

(then angry)

But I *do* have the language and I am *pithy* and *precise.* Eliminate them! Take up the cudgels, and don't cry, and don't hang your head. Kill them,

(soft, trancelike, almost evangelical)

Kill every last one. Kill every living thing, so nothing remains, *nothing,* nothing, kill *every*thing, kill *everyone,* then sow the earth with *salt* – sew it up like they did with Carthage – so nothing grows there ever *ever* again.

(after a short pause; smiles brightly)

My mother used to say that to me. About relationships – we were talking about marriage I think. And she said that even the most intimate relationships, no matter what – your husband, your children – that these were all triangles. That there's no such thing as a couple, that there's always a third person. There's always someone who's *necessary* to the relationship but also *excluded* from it. Love, she taught me, is double sided. So to speak.

So I suppose I do care about foreigners, political prisoners, murderers, terrorists –I believe they have value – not innate value, but the value I assign them. Inasmuch as they are the other side of my relationship with the people I love.

I'm indifferent to *those* people and that indifference is what makes it possible for me to be partial to other people. I think that's what love is.

(She glances over at the sculpture.)

"Das Ding"

The Germans have all these words for things that in America we don't have.

(beat – then to us)

I mean it is sort of horrifying.

(pause)

But I do think it's a work of art.